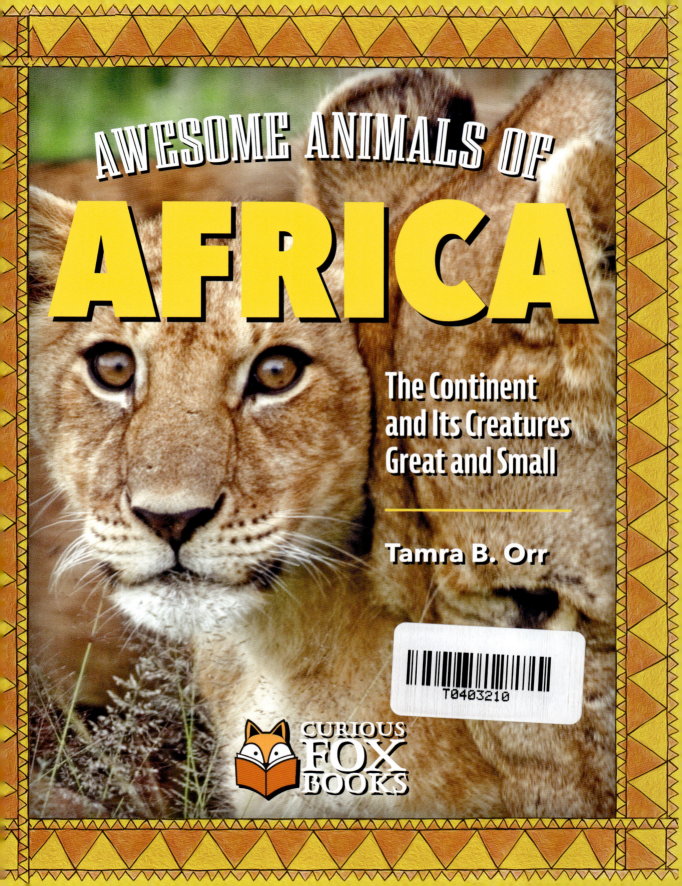

AWESOME ANIMALS OF AFRICA

The Continent and Its Creatures Great and Small

Tamra B. Orr

CURIOUS FOX BOOKS

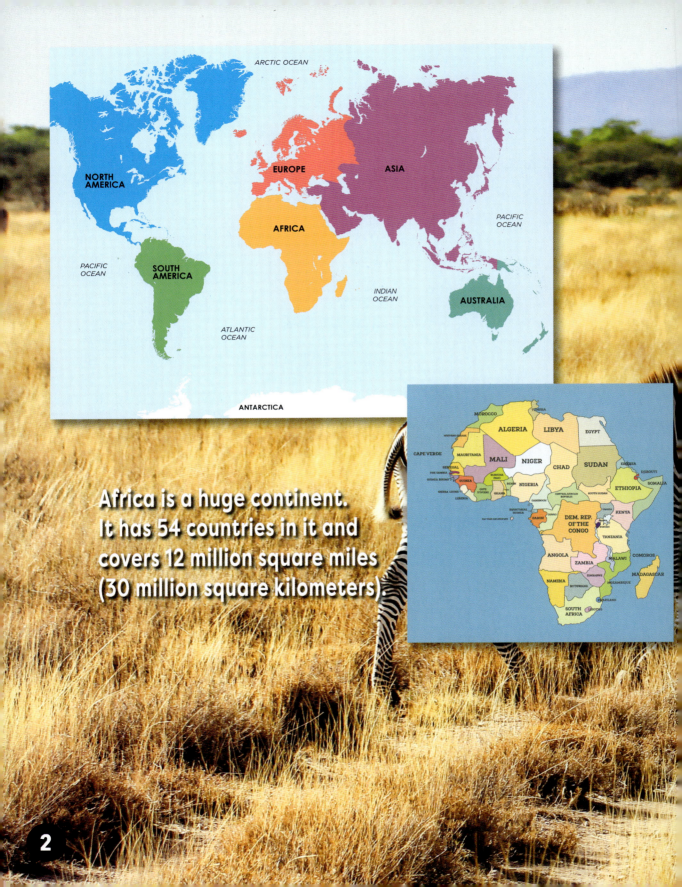

Africa is a huge continent. It has 54 countries in it and covers 12 million square miles (30 million square kilometers).

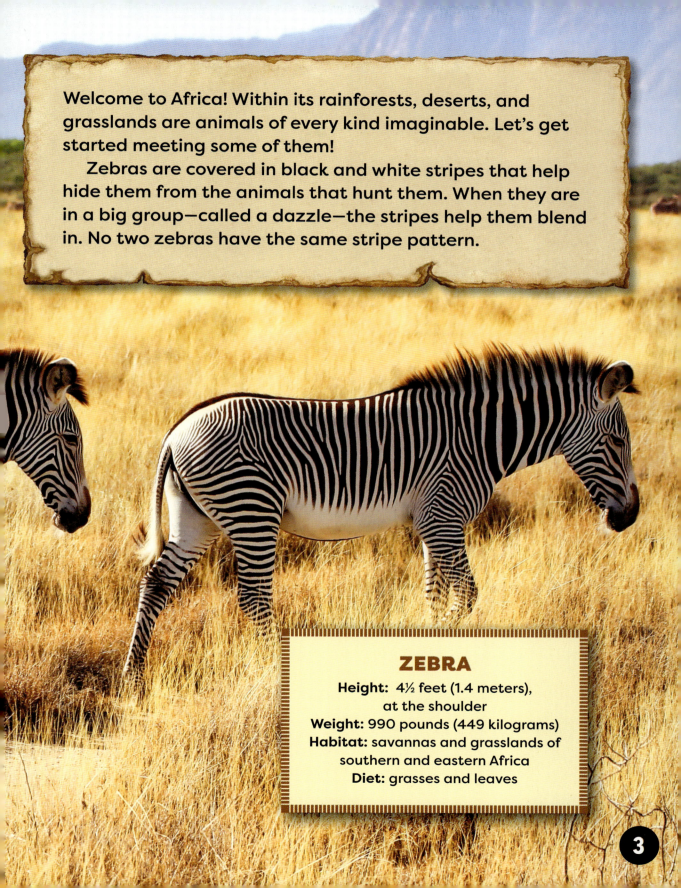

Welcome to Africa! Within its rainforests, deserts, and grasslands are animals of every kind imaginable. Let's get started meeting some of them!

Zebras are covered in black and white stripes that help hide them from the animals that hunt them. When they are in a big group—called a dazzle—the stripes help them blend in. No two zebras have the same stripe pattern.

ZEBRA
Height: 4½ feet (1.4 meters), at the shoulder
Weight: 990 pounds (449 kilograms)
Habitat: savannas and grasslands of southern and eastern Africa
Diet: grasses and leaves

Africa has vast deserts like the Kalahari (ka-la-HAR-ee) and the Sahara (sah-HAYR-ah). This is where dromedary (DRAH-meh-dehr-ee) camels live. Their thick brown coat reflects sunlight, which helps them stay cool. Their humps hold fat that helps them walk a long time without eating or drinking.

DROMEDARY CAMEL
Height: 8 feet (2.4 meters), at the shoulder
Weight: 1,520 pounds (689 kilograms)
Habitat: deserts of northern Africa
Diet: grasses, shrubs, and grains

Lions live in family groups called prides. These big cats love to sleep as much as 20 hours a day. The female lion will hunt for food while the male lion will protect the pride. Lions use their roar to talk to other lions, especially over long distances. A lion's roar can be heard up to 3 miles (4.8 kilometers) away.

LION

Length: 10 feet (3 meters), including tail
Weight: 500 pounds (227 kilograms)
Habitat: grasslands and plains of western, central, and southern Africa
Diet: wildebeests, zebras, and antelopes

The lion is not the most dangerous animal in Africa. That is the hippopotamus. The hippo spends most of its time in the water. It doesn't want anyone coming into its territory. Hippos often knock boats over by ramming into them. They also have very sharp teeth.

HIPPOPOTAMUS

Length: 16½ feet (5 meters)
Weight: 4,000 pounds (1,800 kilograms)
Habitat: rivers and lakes of western, central, and southern Africa
Diet: grasses

The elephants of Africa are the world's largest living land mammals. They send messages to each other over great distances by rumbling. The rumble is too quiet for humans to hear, but other elephants can hear it up to 12 miles (19 kilometers) away. An elephant will bathe in mud or dirt to protect its skin from bugs.

AFRICAN ELEPHANT
Height: 13 feet (4 meters)
Weight: 14,000 pounds (6,000 kilograms)
Habitat: scrubland and forests of western, central, and southern Africa
Diet: leaves, barks, and roots

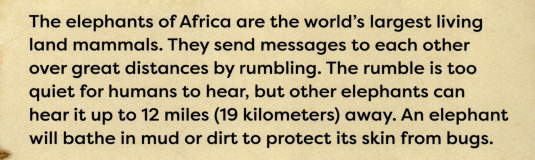

The Asian elephant, shown here, has smaller ears than the African elephant.

The giraffe is the world's tallest land animal. Giraffes can eat leaves from trees that other creatures can't reach. Their long tongues can carefully pull the leaves off the branches. They fill their bellies with about 75 pounds (34 kilograms) of leaves in a day. However, giraffes need to do some gymnastics to drink!

GIRAFFE

Height: 18 feet (5.5 meters)
Weight: 3,000 pounds (1,360 kilograms)
Habitat: savannas of western, eastern, and southern Africa
Diet: leaves, grasses, and fruits

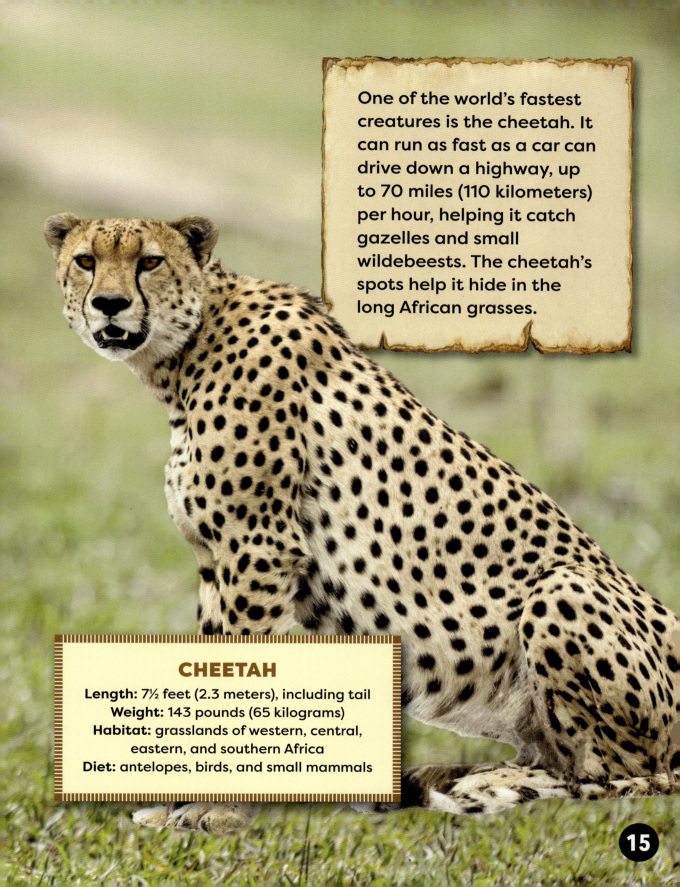

One of the world's fastest creatures is the cheetah. It can run as fast as a car can drive down a highway, up to 70 miles (110 kilometers) per hour, helping it catch gazelles and small wildebeests. The cheetah's spots help it hide in the long African grasses.

CHEETAH
Length: 7½ feet (2.3 meters), including tail
Weight: 143 pounds (65 kilograms)
Habitat: grasslands of western, central, eastern, and southern Africa
Diet: antelopes, birds, and small mammals

Antelope are deer-like creatures. There are many kinds of antelopes in Africa, including impalas (im-PAL-ahz) and wildebeests (WIL-duh-beasts). They are always on the move, migrating from one place to another.

BLUE WILDEBEEST

Height: 5 feet (1.5 meters), at the shoulder
Weight: 550 pounds (249 kilograms)
Habitat: grasslands and mountains of southern Africa
Diet: grasses and leaves

IMPALA

Length: 3 feet (1 meter), at the shoulder
Weight: 168 pounds (76 kilograms)
Habitat: grasslands and forests of eastern and southern Africa
Diet: leaves, grasses, and fruits

Chimpanzees are very smart. These apes use tools to do things like collect insects or crack nuts to eat. Gorillas may look fierce, but they are shy and like to stay in their forest homes. The biggest of the group becomes the leader. Adult male gorillas are called silverbacks for the gray hair they get at age 12 to 15.

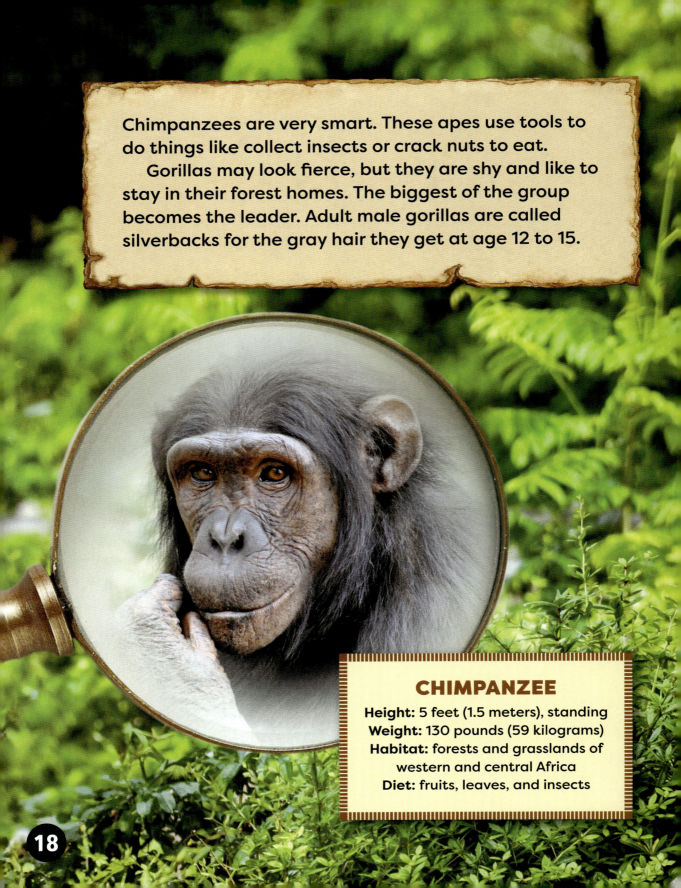

CHIMPANZEE
Height: 5 feet (1.5 meters), standing
Weight: 130 pounds (59 kilograms)
Habitat: forests and grasslands of western and central Africa
Diet: fruits, leaves, and insects

GORILLA
Height: 6 feet (1.8 meters), standing
Weight: 500 pounds (227 kilograms)
Habitat: forests and mountains of central Africa
Diet: fruits and leaves

MANDRILL
Length: 3½ feet (1 meter), including tail
Weight: 70 pounds (32 kilograms)
Habitat: rainforests of central Africa
Diet: fruits, leaves, insects, and reptiles

Mandrills are the largest monkeys in the world. They have pouches in their cheeks that they can stuff with food to eat later.

There are over 100 different types of lemurs. They all come from the island of Madagascar. Lemurs live in the trees and can leap 30 feet (9 meters) to go from branch to branch.

RING-TAILED LEMUR
Length: 18 inches (46 centimeters), not including tail
Weight: 6 pounds (2.7 kilograms)
Habitat: forests of southwestern Madagascar
Diet: fruits, leaves, insects, birds, and reptiles

Ostriches are the world's largest birds. They cannot fly, but they can sprint at 43 miles (69 kilometers) per hour. That's too fast for a car to drive in a school zone!

OSTRICH
Height: 9 feet (2.7 meters)
Weight: 290 pounds (132 kilograms)
Habitat: savannas and deserts of western, eastern, and southern Africa
Diet: fruits, leaves, insects, reptiles, and small mammals

AFRICAN GRAY PARROT
Wingspan: 20 inches (51 centimeters)
Weight: 22 ounces (624 grams)
Habitat: forests of western and central Africa
Diet: fruits, seeds, and nuts

The African gray parrot can imitate almost any sound, including the human voice. It can say whole sentences, and even chirp, beep, and meow.

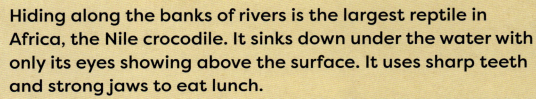

Hiding along the banks of rivers is the largest reptile in Africa, the Nile crocodile. It sinks down under the water with only its eyes showing above the surface. It uses sharp teeth and strong jaws to eat lunch.

The black mamba is one of the most dangerous snakes in Africa. It has enough venom to kill a large animal. The "black" in its name refers to the inside of its mouth.

NILE CROCODILE

Length: 15 feet (4.6 meters), including tail
Weight: 1,650 pounds (748 kilograms)
Habitat: lakes, rivers, and swamps of western Madagascar and western, eastern, and central Africa
Diet: fish, birds, wildebeests, and antelopes

BLACK MAMBA

Length: 8 feet (2.4 meters)
Weight: 2½ pounds (1.6 kilograms)
Habitat: savannas and scrublands of central and southern Africa
Diet: birds and small mammals

Many fearsome insects dwell in Africa. Driver ants have strong pincers. Some African tribes use their snapping heads like stitches to close up open wounds.

East African lowland honey bees are territorial about their hives. They will send twice as many bees to protect them as other types of honeybees.

DRIVER ANT
Length: ½ inch (1.5 centimeter)
Habitat: rainforests, scrublands, and grasslands of central and eastern Africa
Diet: insects, worms, rodents, and small birds

EAST AFRICAN LOWLAND HONEY BEE
Length: ⅔ inch (1.7 centimeters)
Habitat: grasslands and savannas of eastern and southern Africa
Diet: pollen and nectar

BLACK FAT-TAILED SCORPION
Length: 2½ inch (6.4 centimeters)
Habitat: deserts of western and northern Africa
Diet: insects, lizards, and small mammals

The black fat-tailed scorpion is found in the desert regions of North Africa. Its venom is among the deadliest in the world. The black fat-tailed scorpion lives in warm, dry areas.

WHITE RHINOCEROS
Length: 12 feet (3.7 meters)
Weight: 5,000 pounds (2,200 kilograms)
Habitat: grasslands and savannas of central and southern Africa
Diet: grasses

The rhinoceros is the second-largest land animal in the world, after the elephant. A rhino's mighty horn is made of the same stuff as our hair and fingernails.

Many amazing animals call Africa home. It's easy to see why. Africa has mountains, rainforests, savannas, rivers, and deserts— all on one continent!

FURTHER READING

Books

Berkes, Marianne. *Over in the Grasslands: On an African Savanna*. Nevada City, CA: Dawn Publications, 2016.

Owings, Lisa. *Meet a Baby Hippo*. Minneapolis, MN: Lerner Publications, 2015.

Rustad, Martha. *African Animals*. North Mankato, MN: Capstone Books, 2014.

Schaefer, Lola. *Run for Your Life! Predators and Prey on the African Savanna*. New York: Holiday House, 2016.

Websites

A to Z Kids Stuff: Africa
http://www.atozkidsstuff.com/africa.html

Africam
http://www.africam.com

Explore: African Watering Hole Animal Camera
http://explore.org/livecams/african-wildlife/african-watering-hole-animal-camera

National Geographic Kids: South Africa
http://kids.nationalgeographic.com/explore/countries/south-africa

GLOSSARY

continent (KON-teh-nent)—One of the great divisions of land.
desert (DEZ-ert)—Area where it does not rain very often.
grassland—Land covered in grasses and low green plants.
imitate (IM-eh-tayt)—Copy.
mammal (MAM-al)—Warm-blooded animal with hair or fur.
mane—Hair on an animal's neck.
plain—Flat area of land.
pouches—Pockets.
rainforest—Area where it rains daily.
savanna (suh-VAN-uh)—A flat grassland in a tropical area.
scrubland—Area that is hot but has more plants than a desert.
territory (TAIR-ih-tor-ee)—Area an animal lives in.
venom (VEN-um)—Poison produced by an animal.

PHOTO CREDITS

Inside front cover and back cover—Shutterstock/ruboart; p. 1—David Dennis; pp. 2-3—Shutterstock/CK-TravelPhotos; p. 2 (world map)—Shutterstock/Maxger; p. 2 (country map)—Shutterstock/Art-is-Power; pp. 4-5—Grand Parc-Bordeaux, France; pp. 6-7—Shutterstock/Halit Omer; pp. 8-9—Shutterstock/Adwo; p. 9 (inset)—Shutterstock/Tomas Drahos; pp. 10-11—Shutterstock/vannoyphotography; p. 11 (inset)—Shutterstock/WildWoodMan; p. 12 (inset)—Shutterstock/Rikhil Shah; pp. 12-13—Shutterstock/Paul Banton; pp. 14-15—Shutterstock/Jayaprasanna T.L; p. 15 (sitting cheetah) Shutterstock/GoodFocused; pp. 16-17—Shutterstock/EcoPrint; p. 17 (impala)—Shutterstock/Abhishek Raviya; p. 18 (chimpanzee)—Afrika Force; pp. 18-19—Shutterstock/Hung Chung Chih; p. 20 (mandrill)—Shutterstock/Robalito; pp. 20-21—Shutterstock/Ondrej_Novotny_92; p. 22(ostrich)—Bernard DuPont; pp. 22-23—Shutterstock/Pazargic Liviu; pp. 24-25—Shutterstock/diegooscar01; p. 25 (black mamba)—Shutterstock/NickEvansKZN; p. 26 (driver ant)—Shutterstock/feathercollector; p. 26 (killer bee)—Jeffery W. Lotz; pp. 26-27—Shutterstock/RB Punnad; pp. 28-29—Frank Shutterstock/Dirk M. de Boer; inside back cover—Shutterstock/ruboart.
All other photos—Public Domain. Every measure has been taken to find all copyright holders of material used in this book. In the event any mistakes or omissions have happened within, attempts to correct them will be made in future editions of the book.

CHECK OUT THE OTHER BOOKS IN THE AWESOME ANIMALS SERIES

Awesome Animals of Antarctica
Awesome Animals of Asia
Awesome Animals of Australia
Awesome Animals of Europe and the United Kingdom
Awesome Animals of North America
Awesome Animals of South America

© 2024 by Curious Fox Books™, an imprint of Fox Chapel Publishing Company, Inc., 903 Square Street, Mount Joy, PA 17552.

Awesome Animals of Africa is a revision of *The Animals of Africa*, published in 2017 by Purple Toad Publishing, Inc. Reproduction of its contents is strictly prohibited without written permission from the rights holder.

Paperback ISBN 979-8-89094-103-9
Hardcover ISBN 979-8-89094-104-6

Library of Congress Control Number: 2024933085

To learn more about the other great books from Fox Chapel Publishing, or to find a retailer near you, call toll-free 800-457-9112 or visit us at *www.FoxChapelPublishing.com*.

We are always looking for talented authors. To submit an idea, please send a brief inquiry to acquisitions@foxchapelpublishing.com.

Fox Chapel Publishing makes every effort to use environmentally friendly paper for printing.

Printed in China